MW00947648

A Star for a King

ISBN 978-1-0980-8482-0 (paperback)
ISBN 978-1-0980-7297-1 (hardcover)
ISBN 978-1-0980-7298-8 (digital)

Copyright © 2021 by Linda Fitzgerald

All rights reserved. No part of this publication may be reproduced, distributed, or transmitted in any form or by any means, including photocopying, recording, or other electronic or mechanical methods without the prior written permission of the publisher. For permission requests, solicit the publisher via the address below.

Christian Faith Publishing, Inc.
832 Park Avenue
Meadville, PA 16335
www.christianfaithpublishing.com

Printed in the United States of America

A Star for a King

Linda Fitzgerald

In the Worlds of Creation, creation began. It had no beginning and no ending. Within this creation of volcanoes spilling hot lava into empty space, waters slamming and booming across a newly formed planet, and fireballs exploding particles of dust dancing all around, animals, plants, and human spirits experienced a beginning. As each unique creation came forth to stand before God, all were endowed with special gifts and purposes. Some it was to dance, some to sing, some to write, some to paint, some to laugh, some to serve. There

were millions of gifts to hand out on Creation Day. Each gift was unique in that it amplified the gifts of all the others. Each spiritual creation marveled in his or her personal gifts presented to them by God.

It was in this world of beauty and love that Abana came into being. She was a star placed in the Heavens and was given the gift of Light. Those beautiful little Lights that shine like diamonds in the sky that give the human race reason to smile and dream of things beyond and great. Upon receiving her spirit form, God looked at Abana with eyes that watered like the seas.

Abana asked God, "Why do your eyes flow like oceans and rivers? Do I make you sad? Am I a failed creation?"

God placed his finger on Abana's ray and looked upon her with moved compassion. "Oh, Abana, you are not a failed creation. Your purpose is yet to be discovered. When you do find who you are to become, you will have my eyes to see. What a glorious scene will that be when you use your spiritual eyes to penetrate deep into your being and worth. I have given you the Gift of Light and Truth. Your Light will burn bright within my Son. But your Gift will be bestowed upon you when the time is right. For now, you will offer comfort to Sun and Cloud."

She wrinkled her nose and pursed her lips at this thought. Offering comfort to Sun and Cloud served no real purpose for humanity. Seriously, she was to spend her time hiding behind Cloud and Sun? Not to shine or offer light. Her mind whispered to her, *Are you okay with this? You are not to be seen. What purpose is there in being a star if the light is turned off?* She stomped her foot, walked away, and vowed to never return again to Creation Day. Just like mankind creations, Abana did not hear the whisperings of the Spirit. She did not see or accept her foreordination.

Therefore she left Creation Day in a state of confusion and went to visit her mother, Polaris. Her voice burned through the air, "Why is it that my purpose is to offer comfort to Sun and Cloud. This does not move people to do good or to change. Why am I to be a star? Stars do not serve any purpose at all other than to have people dream. Why can't I have the power to make mountains for men to climb or seas for men to fish and provide food. Or even motivation for humans to create and invent. Stars! We are all the same. We dot the sky with blue dots at night. But me, I do not even shine. I hide behind Sun and Cloud. No one ever sees me. I just do not exist. Why did God give me this gift? It is of no worth especially if I have no light!"

Her mother, Polaris, looked on with great sadness upon hearing her daughter complain.

Her light flickered in the deep blackness of Abana's heart. Wisely she told her daughter, "Someday you will do a great work. Your starlight will provide happiness and joy when the time is right. Be patient, Abana, and you will see what God has designed for you. I had to grow and learn before I could navigate ships on the great seas. Remember, you need to grow and experience."

"Yeah, right!" Abana replied, head hung low and rays dipping just a bit closer to Earth's surface. "My starlight is not even seen. I am kept hidden behind Cloud and Sun. Stars provide entertainment for dreamers who have no purpose or mission. I am to entertain Cloud and Sun. My friends Aurora and Borealis put on a beautiful color display as the Northern Lights. As they pop, break, and lock ending with the circular dance, colors are presented across the sky that provide a movie of various hues and beauty for those looking up. Stars have no purpose."

"My sweet little Abana. You are young. Your star power has yet to be developed. For now, patience, little one. And when the hour comes, you will know and will be ready to flash radiance across the sky."

Abana vehemently shook her head and blankly gazed at the star creations. Each star appeared the same to her. She glumly responded, "Can you not see? They do not move. They do not make noise. They just sit there in the sky. Silly, silly stars. But my plight is worse than that as I hide behind Sun and Cloud." As she streaked across the darkness, tears flowed from her heavy eyes. She hated the gift that God had bestowed upon her. Hating her mother for not giving her the comfort she so desperately needed.

For the next few centuries, she sat with Cloud and Sun. She would direct them as to when to appear and when to hide. She listened to their stories about giving warmth, life, and shade to all of the inhabitants of Earth. Abana would cry herself to sleep when her chores were complete. It was the same thing, day in and day out. Boring! There has to be more.

There must be more, she thought. Yet each day started the same and ended the same. She directed Sun to rise and set. Her tears signaled Cloud to water and replenish the Earth. Abana would gaze in the night at the millions of stars that shone brightly high above the world and dream of a better life. Abana continued to assist Sun and Cloud, yet joy alluded her. Being tired from her days work, Abana closed her eyes and dreamed about Creation Day. She saw God standing before all his creations. She heard him bless each with special gifts. Abana's heart leapt from deep within when she heard his voice say, "Unto all I give the gift of joy. This gift you must seek and find in your journey. It does not come freely." A smile formed on her lips, as she awoke. Creation Day made her feel happy, but reality did not. At that a tear slipped from her eyes and Cloud poured down rain. *At least I can keep Cloud and Sun happy and assist with their gifts*, she thought. *Still, I think God forgot to sprinkle joy into my being. Perhaps my gift is sadness. Maybe my calling is to be drenched in despair. I believe God has forgotten me among the billions of stars in the sky. I do not know where to turn for direction.*

During this deep pondering, Cloud began to pour rain and Sun hid. All the Earth felt her sadness and groaned hopelessly. Not from Abana's depression, but because she forgot to whom to turn, she forgot her Gift. Her most precious Gift of proclaiming the birth of Christ.

Neglecting prayer as an option, she decided to visit her friends Borealis and Aurora. She secretly hoped that they would be able to take a break from their dance, listen, and comfort her. Talking out loud, Abana whispered to her heart, "I know that their beauty will give me joy. I cannot go on like this any longer. I know this is my purpose, still I think I will visit my friends." She tiptoed around Cloud and Sun and ran to the north, following the light from her mother, Polaris.

With only the light that Polaris provided, Abana tripped and dipped along the galaxy. She plunged into the Milky Way, tumbling in a circular motion.

"Where are you headed?" asked the Milky Way.

"I am going to the Northern Lights to play" was her reply as she somersaulted through the vast stars.

Milky Way started to giggle. It tinkled and echoed in the darkness. "How will you get there with no light? Are you a burned-out star?" Milky Way continued to taunt. "No light! No light? What good are you with no light? I have millions of stars that light and roll and tumble in circular fashion. And you! You are nothing. You simply fade away into the night sky." The tinkling giggles rang in the icy air and sent Abana flying into the galaxy and further away from Polaris's light.

Abana shivered in the cold. She could feel her shell begin to freeze. There was no light. She was plummeting from the sky. Rolling, flipping, while debris hit her from all sides. She screamed into the night sky. "Help me! Mother Polaris, shine your light that I might get to my friends! I know they can answer my question. I know they can bring happiness to my star within!"

Just then, Polaris peaked above the galaxy and guided Abana to the Northern Lights where Aurora and Borealis create a magical land of dance and light. Polaris hoped her daughter would find the joy that she so desperately sought.

Abana floated in the sky as she watched the spectacular scene created by her two friends Aurora and Borealis. They painted the sky with brilliant greens, blues, purples, orange, and colors in-betweens. She clapped her rays in delight at the wonderful scene. Her sorrow seemed to float away as her friends delighted her with a scene of beauty and light.

Upon hearing the clapping, Borealis and Aurora stopped, and with bewilderment, they asked, "Why are you here? Do you not remember your purpose given to you on Creation Day? You should not be here, but following the path given to you by our Maker and Creator?"

Abana bowed low and a trickle of water fell from her rays. "I thought you would be happy to see me. Have you forgotten our friendship in the Worlds of Creation? We danced and played."

Aurora's colors began to melt together as one as she replied to Abana, "You, my friend, have forgotten how to be humble. You are breaking up the course of the plan and orb of all things. We do miss you. We do remember our play. Play was yesterday. Now we need to focus on our purpose and keeping the planet in motion."

Borealis chimed in, "You have to get back! The Son is coming, and your part is crucial. Father is angry that you have left your position. His Son is soon to come."

"What do you mean? The sun rises and shines without needing me. I have seen it here as well. I thought you were my friends."

Then Aurora and Borealis whispered to her, "Do you not remember the plan? God is sending His Son. And you are to shine brightly to show all mankind when he is born. They will know of his birthplace by your light!"

Abana hissed within her dark shadows, "Have you not noticed I have no light. I have not been blessed with light or a purpose. I was never given a gift as the others. I came here to find peace. I came here to find purpose. All I have found is hate and anger. I needed you, and you have turned away from me. You have betrayed me!" She turned to slide back to Sun and Cloud.

This was a stupid, stupid idea to come here. Me? Thinking my friends would care!

Together the Northern Lights reached out to encircle her in their light, but the silence caused them to pause, and fear fell upon their space. At that moment, a huge thunderbolt erupted through the sky. It pitched Abana through the atmosphere. Aurora's and Borealis' colors froze.

The voice spoke again, this time as the whispering of leaves floating upon the ground. "Abana, Christ Jesus the Redeemer of all Mankind, My beloved Son, is to be born tomorrow and that is when you will be presented with your light. I bestowed upon you at Creation Day the Gift of Light and Truth. It is on the morrow that your Light will be fully formed, and you will show all mankind the way to Him Who Saves. My beautiful Abana, I have given you one of my greatest gifts. You have been so busy feeling sorry for yourself that you forgot to seek, ask, look, study, and find. The answer was within you, waiting for you to observe and grasp as the veil slowly peeled away and allowed you to see and remember Creation Day in the Stellar Nursery. Your faithful friends remembered and gently reminded you. Do not find fault with them."

Remembrance floated around her being and a bit of the veil lifted enough for her to be given a vision. Within this vision-dream, she saw God and heard His words once again. "You will be given the gift of Truth and Light." The words echoed over and over her fragments, "You will be given the gift of Truth and Light. It must develop. It must grow. And when the time is right, your light will radiate the whole Earth." She saw the Father's hand's placed on her photosphere and seal this blessing upon her.

When the vision lifted, Abana was tearful. Quivering she quietly spoke, "Is it too late? Is there forgiveness for me? I have kept a cold dark space and not allowed the lights to burn within my core. I have not prayed and sought guidance. I offended Him who will be born to save. I refused to see and accept my purpose. I was taught by my Father and Mother. I chose to close my ears. My clouded vison kept me from seeing the guile that ran deep within my soul. Oh, Father, forgive me!

I cannot comprehend the sin as I felt I was without guile, but guile runs deep within my core." She dipped and curved her rays at His feet.

With compassion, the Father responded, "Oh my sweet, Abana. Your humility is accepted. Your repentance is accepted. Forgiveness is given to you by Me and Him who will save all from sin. Now you must hurry as the time is near at hand."

Abana raised her face to Him and humbly accepted her calling given to her on Creation Day in the Stellar Nursery. She streaked across the night sky, hoping her light would not burn out as she could feel its warmth floating with in. She prayed that she would not be a shooting star, too soon to lose her light and to be replaced because of her unwillingness to take upon her the calling bestowed upon her. She did not want another to be given her gift. Abana desired with her whole being to be given the opportunity to complete her purpose on Earth. Would she lose this all because she was prideful and unteachable? The whole time she was praying, "Father, forgive me. Jesus, forgive me. Allow me to give this gift for all mankind. Allow me to be the one to show men the way to Him."

At this moment, she felt a peace and calm cover her like a warm blanket. Abana knew the Father was sending a reminder that she had been forgiven. The corners of her rays turned up as peace, and joy filled her soul.

Finally, she arrived at the stable. She encircled the manger three times dropping bits of light upon the Child and His birthplace. She presented to Him her Gift, given to her by Him. Her light shone brighter than that of Polaris and the Celestial realm that she inhabited because of His love. It shone brighter than all the millions of stars that painted the sky that day and night. It was as though night could not penetrate for all hate, all dark, all evil had significantly been erased from all creation kind. Within her rays, she brought with her the blessing of the Light of Christ for He had filled her being with His Light as he stretched his tiny hands toward her.

His Light penetrated deep within her beams. Abana felt meek, lowly, and small compared to the Light He had given her that day.

The Celestial Lights glowed allowing all the world, both Great and Small to know of His birth.

She guided the shepherds, the wise men, the poor, the meek, the lost, the hopeful—she guided all to come and see. Come and adore. Come and worship. Come and sing Hosanna from Angels on High. And they came bringing gifts of gold, frankincense, myrrh, and love. They came singing, worshipping, adoring; they came full of hope and wonder. Still Abana's light shone. It glowed brightly for all of those that believed and hid for those who did not.

Abana showered Mary and Joseph with comforting calm. Her radiant beams warmed the Baby Jesus as His gratitude for her gift skipped all around the Celestial Heavens.

Abana's tears began to flow for the heat and the energy was weighing heavy upon her. She knew in her heart that her time was ending. She had one last gift to give all mankind, all creations everywhere. When the hour came that the Christ child had to flee with His mother Mary and Joseph, Abana sparked a fire never seen before by man or any of God's creations. It lit the world ablaze, and it filled each being that had existed, that would yet exist, and that did exist. She helped to give the Light of Christ to all who believed as He filled her with Light. Abana filled the Earth with His Light as she and Angels proclaimed the birth of Christ to all! She aided Christ by sharing His Light with the world. Abana's light reminds us all of Christ and the Light He shares with those who believe, trust, and follow Him.

Where did that starlight go on that day? It went into the hearts of all creation. It lit up the world with Christ's Light. It shone around the Christ child as Heavenly Celestial beams. It is the Light given to all to know of Him and His love. Jesus shares that Light with us all! May the Light of Christ always burn within your bosom and your homes!

PHOTO

About the Author

Linda A. Fitzgerald has spent most of her life teaching students literature, creative writing, English, and Spanish. She has taught in Utah, Colorado, and Arizona schools. At present, she is a Head Start assistant teacher for pre-five-year-olds. Linda received a BA degree in language with an emphasis in Spanish and, a Secondary Education Certificate at Southern Utah State University in Cedar City, Utah, and a Special Education Certificate through Weber State University, Ogden, Utah. While attending Southern Utah State College, she won an essay-scholarship award sponsored by the university faculty spouses. Linda was a journalist for a religious newspaper in which one of her stories about a rodeo cowboy who was miraculously healed from a neck injury when he fell off his horse made the front page. She is married to her best friend, Michael Fitzgerald. Together they have five children, nine grandchildren, and three great-grandchildren. Linda and her husband are active members of the Church of Jesus Christ of Latter-Day Saints; having served various callings over the years.

Currently Linda and her husband, Michael, live in Sandy, Utah.